THE RATS' DAUGHTER

told and illustrated by J O E L C O O K

Caroline House

B O Y D S M I L L S P R E S S

Stories of unquenchable ambition are told in every language, and many tales use animals cynically to represent humans. The choice of animals often says as much as their actions.

The story in this book springs mostly from "The Husband of the Rat's Daughter" as told by Andrew and Leonora Lang in *The Brown Fairy Book* of 1904.

Copyright © 1993 by Joel Cook
All rights reserved

Published by Caroline House
Boyds Mills Press, Inc.
A Highlights Company
910 Church Street, Honesdale, Pennsylvania 18431

Publisher Cataloging-in-Publication Data
Cook, Joel.
The rats' daughter / told and illustrated by Joel Cook.—1st ed.
[32] p. : col. ill. ; cm.
An adaptation of "The Husband of the Rat's Daughter" from *The Brown Fairy Book*, 1904.
Summary: A classic tale of a mother's search for the perfect husband for her daughter; the best mate is the one she ignored.
ISBN 1-56397-140-2
1. Folklore—Juvenile literature. 2. Rats—Juvenile fiction. [1. Folklore. 2. Rats—Fiction.] I. Title.
398.2—dc20   1993
Library of Congress Catalog Card Number: 92-71871

First edition, 1993
The text of this book is set in 16-point Cochin.
The illustrations are done in colored pencil.
Distributed by St. Martin's Press
Printed in the United States of America

1 3 5 7 9 10 8 6 4 2

THE RATS' DAUGHTER

Dedicated to a dear friend,
though indeed she always preferred *mice*.

Once there were two rats, husband and wife,
who came from old and noble families.

Their daughter was the loveliest of rat girls,
and they spared no effort or expense in her education.

No one was better than she at
singing, dancing, gnawing through hard wood,
or running away when big people came near.

Her eyes were bright, her skin shone like satin,
and her pearly teeth were beautifully pointed.

Her parents knew she'd make a brilliant marriage
and soon began to look for a suitable husband.

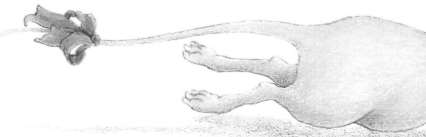

Her father, a true rat from nose to tail,
wanted her to marry a fine young rat,
whose family was the oldest and noblest around.

Her mother had other ideas.
"My child," she proclaimed, "is far too beautiful
and much too talented to marry a mere rat.
My daughter will marry only the best!"

She talked that way, as mothers will,
to anyone who would listen.

What the girl thought, nobody knew.
It was not the rat fashion to care about such things.

Many were the quarrels the husband and wife had about it,
until one day the lady said, "Reach To The Stars is my motto!
My daughter's beauty is above anything on earth,
and I certainly will not accept a
son-in-law who is beneath her!"

"Then you'd better marry her to the sun,"
said her husband in a huff.
"I don't suppose anyone is greater than he."

"Well, I was thinking of it," his wife replied,
"and since you seem to agree, we will visit him tomorrow."

Next morning, after hours spent getting ready,
they set out with their daughter between them.

It was a long journey, but at last . . .

. . . they arrived at the golden palace
where the sun lived.

"Noble king," the mother began, "behold our
beautiful daughter, who is above everything in the world.
Naturally, we seek a son-in-law who, on his side,
is also greatest. Therefore we have come to you."

"I am flattered," replied the sun
(who didn't want to marry anyone at all).
"You honor me, but in one way you are mistaken.
There is one greater than I, and that is the cloud.

Look!"

They looked, and the cloud spread
until it dimmed the sun's light.

"Oh. Well.
Then we will speak to him," said the mother,
and turning to the cloud, she repeated her proposal.

"Indeed," the cloud sighed,
"I am unworthy of anything so charming, but again
you are mistaken. The wind is more powerful than I.

Here, see for yourself."

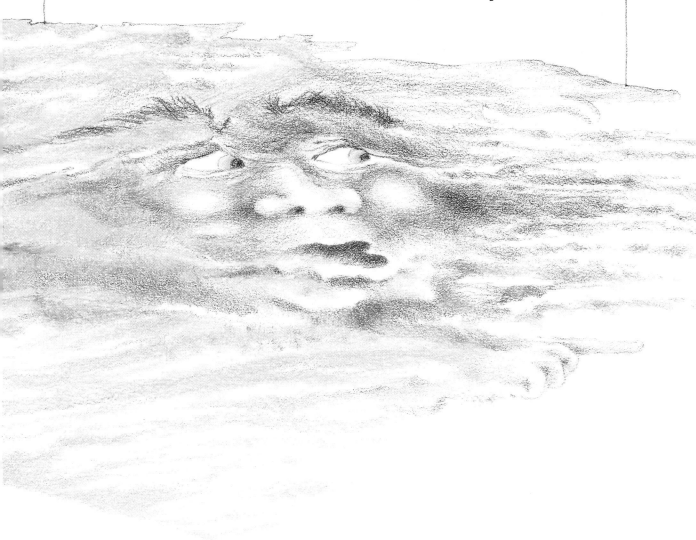

And she did see, for the wind
tossed the cloud across the sky

and tumbled father, mother, and daughter
down to earth.

Then the wind paused beside them,
quieted for a moment by an old wall.
As soon as the mother rat caught her breath,
she began her little speech once more.

The wind interrupted.
"The wall is the proper husband for your daughter.
You have seen for yourself
that he can stop me in my flight."

The mother, who wanted only the best for her child,
turned to speak to the wall.

At that moment, to everyone's surprise,
the daughter spoke first.

"I *won't* marry that ugly old wall!" the girl shouted.
"No, no, no, *no!!*
I would have married the sun, or perhaps the cloud,
or maybe even the wind, because you wanted it,
even though I love only the handsome young rat.
But that horrid old wall, *never!"*

And the wall, though his feelings were hurt,
declared that he had no claim
to the hand of so lovely a girl.
"It's true I can stop the wind,
who can part the clouds,
who can dim the sun,
but the rat can get through me where the wind cannot.
If you want a son-in-law greater than the whole world,
seek him among the rats!"

"What did I tell you?" the husband cried,
and though his wife didn't like being bettered,
she soon decided that if a rat was the best, then
a rat son-in-law was just what she'd always wanted.

The young folk had a splendid wedding,
which was only right;
and they were happy together,
which was fortunate.

And the sun was happy, too, and smiled on them.